Helena Pielichaty (pronounced Pierre-li-hatty) has written numerous books for children, including *Simone's Letters*, which was nominated for the Carnegie Medal, and the popular After School Club series. A long-standing Huddersfield Town supporter, there are few who could write with as much enthusiasm about girls' football. A local girls' under 11s team helps with the inspiration and tactical know-how, but Helena has been an avid fan of women's football for many years. It clearly runs in the family: her aunt was in a women's team in the 1950s and her daughter has been playing since she was ten (she is now twenty-four!). Helena lives in Nottinghamshire with her husband and has two grown-up children.

The Girls FC series

So What If I Hog The Ball?

Helena Pielichaty

WALKER
BOOKS

For Eudy Simelane (1977–2008), captain of the
South African Women's football team

First published 2010 by Walker Books Ltd
87 Vauxhall Walk, London SE11 5HJ

10 9 8 7 6 5 4 3 2 1

Text © 2010 Helena Pielichaty
Cover illustration © 2010 Sonia Leong

The right of Helena Pielichaty to be identified as author
of this work has been asserted by her in accordance with
the Copyright, Designs and Patents Act 1988

This book has been typeset in Helvetica and Handwriter

Printed and bound in Great Britain by Clays Ltd, St Ives plc

British Library Cataloguing in Publication Data:
a catalogue record for this book is available from the British Library

ISBN 978-1-4063-1739-8

www.walker.co.uk

☆ ☆ The Team ☆ ☆

☆ **Megan "Meggo" Fawcett** GOAL

☆ **Petra "Wardy" Ward** DEFENCE

☆ **Lucy "Goose" Skidmore** DEFENCE

☆ **Dylan "Dyl" or "Psycho 1" McNeil** LEFT WING

☆ **Holly "Hols" or "Wonder" Woolcock** DEFENCE

☆ **Veronika "Nika" Kozak** MIDFIELD

☆ **Jenny-Jane "JJ" or "Hoggy" Bayliss** MIDFIELD

☆ **Gemma "Hursty" or "Mod" Hurst** MIDFIELD

☆ **Eve "Akka" Akboh** STRIKER

☆ **Tabinda "Tabby" or "Tabs" Shah** STRIKER/MIDFIELD

☆ **Daisy "Dayz" or "Psycho 2" McNeil** RIGHT WING

☆ **Amy "Minto" or "Lil Posh" Minter** VARIOUS

Official name: Parrs Under 11s, also known as the Parsnips

Ground: Lornton FC, Low Road, Lornton

Capacity: 500

Affiliated to: the Nettie Honeyball Women's League junior division

Sponsors: Sweet Peas Garden Centre, Mowborough

Club colours: red and white; red shirts with white sleeves, white shorts, red socks with white trim

Coach: Hannah Preston

Assistant coach: Katie Regan

☆ ☆ Star Player ☆ ☆

☆ **Age:** nearly 10

☆ **Birthday:** October — you don't need to know
when in October

☆ **School:** been to a few — which one do you
want?

☆ **Position in team:** I'll play anywhere,
but I like playing out wide on the wings
best

☆ **Likes:** footy, especially watching the
Parrs senior team play from my bedroom
window. Telly. Being left alone.

☆ **Dislikes:** my brothers, especially Billy
when he's in a mood and it all kicks off
in our house. Teachers. People who boss
you around. Anything pink.

☆ **Supports:** Parrs (seniors), England,
Millwall FC (they're like my family — nobody
like us but we don't care.)

Jenny-Jane "Hoggy" Bayliss

☆ **Favourite player(s) on team:** Megan 'cos she let me on the team and she's never judged me. Gemma for skill. And Nika's all right too.

☆ **Best football moment:** when we win, of course

☆ **Match preparation:** I turn up early and practise with a tennis ball

☆ **Have you got a lucky mascot or a ritual you have to do before or after a match?** What for? You can go nuts doing that.

☆ **What do you do in your spare time?** Mind my own business

☆ **Favourite book(s):** Foul Play by Tom Palmer

☆ **Favourite band(s):** Aerosmith

☆ **Favourite film:** Transformers

☆ **Favourite TV programme(s):** Wayne Rooney's Street Striker

Pre-match Interview

Wotcha. My name is Jenny-Jane Bayliss
and I play in a girls' football team
called the Parrs Under 11s. It's the
greatest girls' football team in the
world, and if anyone says it isn't
they'll get battered.

I've got to tell you about the start
of the second season. I'm not happy.
There's a lot of family stuff tied up
in that part. Stuff I'd rather forget.
But Megan says not to worry, to tell
it like it happened and it'll all be
fine. I hope she's right. If not, our
Billy's gonna kill me.

Cheers,
Jenny-Jane Bayliss

1

It was half-past eight and the taxi driver was outside the gate, piping his horn like crazy, making it very difficult to concentrate on the weather report.

"Come on, ducky. You'll be late," Mam said, with that wheedling tone in her voice – it never works, so I don't know why she uses it. I glanced away from the TV to find her standing with my backpack in her hands, her thin pencilled-on eyebrows furrowed like corrugated cardboard. "Please, Jenny-Jane!" she begged.

She sounded desperate but I really, *really* didn't want to go to prison today, so I returned to the weather. Temperatures were going to be average for the time of year.

"I'll give you five pounds," Mam said.

"Nope."

"Ten?"

"Mam, you know you're skint. Stop showing yourself up."

She sighed. "All right, Jenny-Jane. I give in. You can stay at home."

"Honest?" I asked, swivelling round to check if her face matched her words. I mean, it usually took a bit more work than that to make her crumble.

She dumped my bag on the kitchen table and nodded. "Honest – if it means it stops that din out there. At this rate that idiot will wake everybody up."

By "everybody" she means Dad and my brothers, Billy and Brendan. None of them works – Dad's on disability and my two brothers are bone-idle – so most mornings they lie in.

"Thanks, Mam, you're a star." I jumped up, my heart soaring as I headed for the door so I could tell the driver to take a hike.

"Mind you…" Mam said, just as I reached for the door handle.

"'Mind you' what?"

"I can't guarantee what mood our Billy'll be in when he wakes up and finds you here."

She had a point. Since he'd come out of the youth offenders' centre, Billy's moods were gruesome. He'd turned into a right psycho. On the other hand, the thought of spending the day with the psychos in Little Alcatraz didn't exactly thrill me to bits, either. This was not a win-win situation.

I looked at Mam, looked at the weather reader, looked at Mam again. Should I stay or should I go? My eye caught the day at the top of the weather chart. Tuesday. It was Tuesday, and Tuesday was football training. That was the clincher. I didn't want to give Billy an excuse for keeping me from going to that. Apart from the match proper, training was the best part of my week. "I suppose I'll go to the prison, then," I grumbled, snatching my bag from the table.

"But if I come home in a body bag, don't say
I didn't warn you."

Mam gave me a relieved smile and reached for
the detergent bottle. "Have a nice day," she called
just before I slammed the door.

2

Half an hour later the taxi driver pulled up outside Mowborough Pupil Referral Unit.
OK, I admit that it's not a prison exactly, but it's near enough. Like one teacher at King John's, my last school, said it's a big step in that direction.

To fool people into thinking it was a normal place for normal kids, the outside of the PRU looked like any school building. You know – flat roof, rows of windows, the few shrubs outside the main entrance trimmed with empty crisp packets. Inside wasn't that bad either – better than King John's, anyway. For starters there were only six in the class. Yep, six – me and five psycho boys. My dad reckoned the unit was better than private school, what with the teacher–pupil ratio and the free taxi ride. That's because he doesn't have to come here, I thought, as I spotted Mrs Kelly, the head warden, coming towards me, a chunky necklace swinging from her chunky neck, her bare arms full of folders.

"Ah! Jenny-Jane," she said. "Just the person I'd like to see. Come into my room for a minute, if you don't mind."

I panicked, wondering if I had anything in my bag I shouldn't have, like one of our nicked mobiles or something. What had I packed that morning? Sarnies for lunch, pencil tin and a tennis ball in case I got chance to do a few keepy-uppies later. Nope. Everything in my bag was legit. I sighed and told myself not to be such a wimp. "Why, Miss? I'm not that late, am I?" I asked.

"Don't worry. It's not about your punctuality." She elbowed open the door to her office and I reluctantly followed her in.

Mrs Kelly told me to sit down. She then took the top file from the pile she'd been carrying and opened it. It had a pink spine.

I hate pink. It's the vilest of all colours. Everyone knows red's best, followed by blue, then white.

"Is that about me?" I asked.

"It is."

"Why's it pink? Because I'm the only girl here?"

"Coincidence," she said, leaning forward so that her necklace collided with the folders. "So, Jenny-Jane, how are you settling in?"

"All right, I suppose." That was if you called sitting in the corner of a classroom watching two teachers trying to control five loopy boys all day "settling in". Three weeks and two days I'd been there, excluding the summer holidays. It felt like three years.

Mrs Kelly gazed at me in a soppy way, which worried me. I wasn't used to being gazed at like that, especially by head teachers. "Look at you. You really shouldn't be here at all, should you?"

Amen to that, I thought.

"We need to get you back into mainstream school as soon as possible, don't we?"

"Not King John's," I told her. "I wouldn't go back there if you paid me."

"No, not King John's," she agreed instantly. "I don't think there's much danger of that."

"Good," I said.

"We'd be looking at one of the other Mowborough primary schools."

"Fair enough."

"But first you have to prove that you're capable of being in a classroom environment without disrupting it – and that's not always been easy for you, has it, Jenny-Jane?"

I shrugged. There wasn't much I could say. The evidence was in front of her, in black and white and triplicate.

"So I'm setting you some targets based on what Mrs Law and Mr Upton have told me..."

Targets? Feeble old targets? She must know I'd been set more of them in my time than Robin Hood. "Go on." I sighed.

Mrs Kelly picked up a loose piece of paper from

the top of my file. "Your target this week will be to mix more," she said. "Can you think of any ways in which you could do that?"

"To be honest, mixing with nutters isn't my thing, Miss," I told her.

The phone rang before she could reply. "You're kidding," she said to whoever was on the other end. "But he knows he's on a final warning... Oh, send him to me straight away. Yes, yes, straight away..." She put the phone down, grunted, then closed my file. "I'm sorry, Jenny-Jane, I'm going to have to leave it there. Problems in the seniors."

"I'm not surprised," I said. "They're even bigger nutters up that end than down this end, from what I've seen."

She drew a breath, then decided not to waste it by denying what I'd said and gave me a full-beam-ahead smile instead. "So you're going to have a think about mixing, aren't you?"

"I'll think about it," I agreed, "but I'm not making no promises."

☆ ☆ ☆

I thought about it all day. I thought about it when
this kid in an Arsenal shirt, Ronnie Parkin, did
nothing but stare at me as he picked at the scab
on his ear and ate the crust. I thought about it
when two of the other nut-jobs kicked off after
lunch and one of them, Clayton White, swept my
stuff off my table with his arm as he passed on his
way to the time-out room. I thought about it when
Mrs Law gave me a book to read that I'd already
read and said, "Read it again, then, dear," like I
was two or something. I thought about it and what
I thought was this: targets are rubbish.

3

At home, I chucked my bag under the stairs and went into the kitchen. Dad, our Brendan and our Billy were sat round the table smoking and drinking tea. Mam was at the sink peeling spuds.

"Ugh! It stinks in here," I complained, wafting my hand in the air at all the smoke.

"It does now you're back," our Billy said.

"Ha, ha."

"Yeah, *ha, ha*, like the service round here. Mam, where's that sugar I asked for ten minutes ago?" Billy demanded.

Mam stopped peeling the potatoes and dashed to the cupboard about two inches from where Billy was sitting. "Sorry, duck, I forgot," she said, handing him the bag of sugar and a spoon.

"Should think so," he muttered.

"Now then, how was school, duck?" Dad asked me.

"Keep telling you, it's not a school, is it? It's a *unit*."

"The unit, then, bossy breeches. How was the unit?"

"What's the opposite of awesome?"

Dad frowned. "Um … I don't know. Pants?"

"Pants. Exactly," I told him, moving his walking-stick so I could sit down. Between you and me, he doesn't really need it. His broken leg healed yonks ago, but he keeps the stick handy in case anyone drops by from Social Services. Once a con artist, always a con artist.

"Did anyone give you any grief?" our Brendan wanted to know. "I'll see to them if they did."

Bren couldn't fight his way out of a crèche, but I appreciated the sentiment. "Nah."

"You shouldn't even be there," Dad grunted, "a smart button like you. You've got more brains than the whole lot of us put together."

I felt the teapot to check how fresh it was and poured myself a brew. "Thanks, Dad, but, let's face it, having more brains than you lot isn't exactly a stretch, is it?"

Dad yawned loudly, showing his gold crowns, then laughed. "True," he said, "very true." He called out to Mam to shove the kettle on. "Time for a top-up," he told her.

"All right, Mick, I'm on it," she said, dropping the potato-peeler again and wiping her hands on her apron.

Billy stuck his oar in then. I'd been wondering when he would. "Bright? Her? She's not that bright or she wouldn't have got excluded, would she?"

"Shurrup," I told him, but in a polite way so he wouldn't start.

"Getting caught nicking a teacher's purse."

"It wasn't just because of that," I mumbled and felt my face burn. The purse had been what

Mr Tattershall, my head teacher, called the Final Straw.

"Rule number one: a Bayliss never gets caught."

"Huh! How come you and Bren have just spent nine months in a youth offenders' centre, then?"

"Watch it, or else," he warned.

I would normally have kept quiet, but the mention of the purse stung too much. I wouldn't even have nicked it if Mam hadn't been crying that morning because hardly any money was coming in. "Or else what, loser?" I retorted.

Billy shot out of his chair as if he'd been zapped by lightning and smashed his hand down on the table, making everything on it bounce. The salt cellar toppled over, Mam dropped the kettle into the sink and I cursed, wishing I'd learn to keep my trap shut. "WHAT? *What did you call me*?" Billy bellowed at the top of his voice, spit flying in all directions.

"Oi, oi, oi," Dad said, using his stick as a barrier between us and motioning to Billy to sit down.

"Calm yourself, son. She didn't mean it."

I held my breath, wondering if Billy'd listen to Dad for once or just go for it and clatter me anyway. Eventually he sat, although his green-flecked eyes kept pinging daggers at me. "She needs to learn to show a bit of respect," he muttered.

"Yes, she does," Mam agreed. "I'm always telling her that."

No you're not, I thought. You're always cleaning or cooking or watching rubbish on telly, that's what you're always doing.

"What's for tea?" I asked, thinking a change of subject might be a good idea.

"Nothing for you, if you don't do as Billy says and show some respect," Mam said.

"Nothing's fine by me. I've got training, anyway."

Billy snorted. "Training! What a joke! She's a right laddie-lass. She should call herself Jamie instead of Jenny."

Brendan laughed. "Jamie-Jane. Nice one."

Nice one. Yeah. Like the lever Billy operates to

make your head go up and down, Brendan, you lame lemming.

Dad leaned forward and patted my knee. "Take no notice of them, ducky. I know it's just a phase you're going through, this boys' stuff. You'll be around to look after me and your mam when we're past it, like the good daughter you are."

"You've no chance," Billy told him. "She'll probably be manning an oil rig."

I hope I am, I thought. Being in the middle of a freezing cold ocean has to be better than being in this smelly kitchen with you lot. I didn't say that, though. I wasn't that stupid. Instead I grabbed a few Babybel cheeses from the fridge and an apple from the fruit bowl and legged it to my bedroom.

"Yeah, off you go, laddie-lass," Billy called out after me.

Upstairs, I dashed straight to my bedroom window. It's what I always do. Go straight to the window. Not that there's anything wrong with my bedroom itself. I've got a state-of-the-art flat-screen TV, a Wii, an Xbox, a PlayStation 3 and stacks of other goodies that have "fallen" from the backs of many lorries over the years, but the window's the thing that always calms me down the most.

It's bound to, seeing as I look out on the best view in the world. It is called Lornton Football Club and it is stunning.

I knelt on the games console under the window, rested my elbows on the sill and gazed at it all. I let my eyes roam round the main pitch, with its pristine green turf and freshly painted white line markings, across to the clubhouse where Mandy, the ace club manageress, lives and works, then finally over to the fly-and-wasp-magnet bottle bank that butts up against the side of the club. Stunning. Every bit of it.

Slowly I peeled away the red wax from the first cheese and took a bite. To think that in an hour's

time I'd be down there. Nothing else mattered.
Being in a unit. Billy's bad moods. Mam's manic
cleaning. Nothing. As long as I had Lornton FC and
the Parrs, everything was hunky-dory.

4

In the end, I couldn't wait even an hour.
I bolted down my nosh, got changed, found
my tennis ball and then slipped out of the house
as quietly as I could, using the side door so no
one would notice me and give me any more
hassle.

I headed round to the smaller pitch behind the
clubhouse. This pitch, where we trained, wasn't in
as good nick as the main one, but I liked it better
because the high hedges on two sides secluded
it from the council estate behind, making it private
and peaceful.

I began to jog round it. The breeze against my
face, and the way my chest filled with energy
when I ran, made me feel light and free and giddy.
I broke into a sprint, my legs pounding along the

side of the field, my arms brushing the hedge as if they were high-fiving every leaf.

After that I practised ball control with the tennis ball. I always carried one with me – ever since Megan lent me her book on Michael Owen, and in it he said to practise with a tennis ball because after that a real ball seems easy. And you know what? The bloke was right. Know what else? Pelé used a grapefruit. Weird or what?

Football, football, football. Love it, love it, love it.

While I practised I listened out for cars arriving, and as soon as I heard the first one I belted towards the car park, guessing it would be Hannah and Katie. They chuckled when they saw me. "Here she is. Miss Keen!"

"Our early girly!" Katie teased.

"Shurrup," I said, automatically following them to the storage shed, where I helped to haul out all the equipment.

"What's new, then?" Hannah asked, passing me a stack of cones.

"Nothing much."

"Good. That's the way we like it, eh?"

"Yup."

Soon everyone else began to arrive. We'd already had a few practices during August, but this was the first one that everybody would – or should – turn up to now the summer holidays were over. Megan and Petra bowled up first, followed by the rest of the squad, all talking nineteen to the dozen. I just let it go over my head. I'm not that interested in small talk. It's a waste of time when we could be playing football.

"Calling JJ! Come in, please!"

I blinked as Megan waved a hand in my face. "What?" I asked.

"Dur! We're comparing new teachers. Five words to sum yours up."

Mr Upton flashed into my head. "Aussie, beard, never wears socks," I said.

"What's he called?" Tabinda asked.

"Mrs O'Shea," I replied, giving the name of the teacher I would have had if I'd still been at King John's, and leaving Tabinda with a puzzled look on her face. Well, there's no point advertising the fact I go to a pupil referral unit, is there? None of this lot would understand.

"Gather round, troops. Loads to get through," Hannah called out.

As everyone formed a rough circle, Daisy and Dylan started doing impressions of aeroplanes. Trust them to muck about from the start. I saw Holly nudge Dylan to pack it in. Dylan looked up at her and nodded, then nudged Daisy. Their arms dropped obediently. Nice one, Holly. It was then that I noticed how much taller she was. She dwarfed the twins. Dwarfed Amy Minter next to her – and they'd been the same height before the summer. Holly was taller and … I frowned … thinner. Where had all her chubby bits gone? That was no good. How was she going to shore up the defence without some bulk about her?

I turned to find Minter gawping. I gawped right back. *She* hadn't changed. She still thought she was Hannah Montana, with her just-so shiny hair and mouth caked in lip-gloss. Yuk. I almost wished our Billy was there to see her; he'd know we weren't all laddie-lasses then.

Next to Minter was Nika, babbling away with Lucy, Eve and Gemma. I automatically glanced down to see if she was wearing the boots I'd given her during the summer tournament at Sherburn Sands. She was, and I felt chuffed. Brendan had nicked them for me ages ago, but they were miles too big so I'd swapped them with Nika's. Hers were well tatty, but they fitted a treat and that was all I cared about.

After that I turned my attention where it belonged – on Hannah. Best coach in the world. *Fact*.

"Nice to see you all again." She beamed at us. "Are you all set for the new season?"

"Yay!" everyone cheered.

"Excellent! New season, new start and, all being well, new away strip. Isn't that right, Tabs?"

Tabinda, whose dad sponsored the team, bent to flick something off her knee. "Uh-huh. It should be here on Saturday."

"Cool. So everyone make sure you get to Gorby Road in plenty of time to try sizes out, especially as half of you have shot up so much. What've you been doing, Wonder? Standing in fertilizer for six weeks?"

Holly flushed. "No," she said.

Another coach might have carried on teasing. Gary Browne, who trains the boys' Under 10s team, for one. I watch them sometimes to check out their drills and I've heard him; he's vicious. Not Hannah, though. She'd already moved on and begun swivelling her hips from side to side in preparation for the warm-up. "I hope you're all fit, because we're going to up the ante over the next few weeks. Reinforce everything we did last season, but introduce new skills too…"

Katie (runner-up best coach – *fact*) took over the spiel. "We want you to start thinking for yourselves more. To develop your own instincts, not just for the ball but also for each other. Football's a team game. There are seven of you on the pitch at a time – seven parts of a whole."

"Like days of the week?" Petra asked.

"Something like that." Katie smiled. "The other thing is we feel it's important that none of you gets too entrenched in one position, so we're going to mix it up a bit, especially in midfield."

I frowned. Mix? What was this sudden fascination everyone had with mixing? First Mrs Kelly, now Katie. One mention of targets and I was walking out.

I wasn't the only one who took offence. "Mix it up? Oh! Even us?" Daisy asked. "Please don't mix it up or we'll be really mixed up and highly muddled again."

"We like the wing game," Dylan added, looking flustered. "It makes us skippy."

"Maybe not you two, then, but everybody else," Hannah said. "So, are we ready, girls?"

"We're ready!"

"Excellent. Spread out…"

And then we began. Warm-ups followed by drills in small groups. Things like quick passing and short passing. Dodging with the ball. Running and changing direction. All good stuff.

We finished off with a six-a-side match, and I hit the side netting once and shot wide twice.

"You could have crossed it!" Eve called out to me a couple of times.

"I will next time," I called back.

Our team won five–three. My legs ached like mad by the end, but I didn't care. I'd enjoyed every second, even though it had gone faster than a blink of an eye.

"Not bad, not bad," Hannah told us. "Your fitness levels aren't too dreadful. You should just about survive on Saturday without collapsing. Right, let's warm down…"

My heart sank. I always hated warming down.
It meant the session was over and I had to go
home again.

5

You don't want to know about the rest of my week. It was just the same old stuff – got up, went to prison, came home, ate, kipped. I won't pretend I did what Mrs Kelly asked and mixed more, but I did stay out of trouble. At King John's I'd have been given a gold medal for that.

Back home, Billy kept out of my face and I kept out of his, though there was a massive fight between him and Brendan on Thursday night – but I was upstairs watching *Total Wipeout*, so I don't know what it was about.

And that was it, more or less, unless you're desperate for information about what meals I had and how many times I wiped my nose – in which case, get a life. So I'm going to cut to Saturday, the important part. Hixton Lees v. the Parrs. 10.30 kick-off. Wicked.

Just so you know, I always get a lift in Hannah's car to away matches – we don't have a car. (There's no point since dad lost his licence.) I was so hyper when Hannah picked me up; I couldn't sit still for one second. "So, what do you reckon? Us to win?" I asked, leaning forward and resting my arms on the back of Katie's headrest.

"Who knows?" Katie replied, slotting in a CD. A screechy woman's voice belted out, with Hannah and Katie making it ten times worse by joining in. What a racket!

"We've got to win. That fluky fourth goal they got last time should never have been allowed," I told them. "That number 21…"

Katie twisted round and tapped my elbow. "Forget past grudges, JJ. Fresh season, fresh start. Just focus on what we said at training, about playing as a team."

"Yes, boss," I said, leaning back and letting

them get on with their head-banging.

Football, football, football. Love it, love it, love it.

Hixton Lees's ground is similar to Lornton's in that
it's smack in the middle of a village. Hannah and
Katie wandered over to talk to their oppos, and I
went to find the changing rooms. I was surprised to
see Tabinda's dad standing by the door, a massive
smirk on his face. For a second I wondered why –
then remembered the away kit.

"Ah! Jenny-Jane! Just the person I wanted to
see," he said.

"Me?"

"You indeed. Don't tell her I've told you this, but
Binda's been a little worried about what you'll think
of the new strip."

"Worried? Why?" I asked.

"My point exactly! I've reassured her that you
and the others'll be as delighted with it as I am!
In you go! Let me know what you think. When
you've got changed I'd love a shot of you and

Binda together, if you don't mind. For the website."
He pulled a digital camera from his pocket and
began pressing buttons.

"You want Minter for photos," I told him. "She's
the poser."

I pushed open the door to find Tabinda sitting
on the bench. She was leaning forward and
fastening her boots. "Oh," she said, looking
alarmed when she saw it was me. "Hi, JJ." She
stood up. "W-what do you think?" She held her
arms out from her sides.

I didn't reply. I wasn't ignoring her, I just couldn't
speak. My voice box had been karate-chopped at
the sight of the new pink away shirt. That's what I
said. *Pink*. Pathetic pink with "Sweet Peas Garden
Centre" written in huge black letters across the
front. The socks were pink too. The shorts were
black, but as far as I was concerned that was
too little, too late. The damage was done. No
wonder Tabinda had been worried. I'd have been
a quivering wreck.

She tugged nervously at her socks. "I know w-what you're thinking," she stuttered. "I tried to persuade Dad to go for purple or something, but he wouldn't listen. This is the nearest shade he could get to 'Gwendoline', his favourite sweet pea."

I heard the door open behind me, and Hannah went, "Ah!" and Katie went, "Tabs! You look ace!"

But Tabinda was still waiting for me to respond. "Dad says to tell anyone who's not happy that an Italian team called Palermo play in pink and so do loads of other teams – men's and women's." When I still didn't say anything she looked pleadingly across at Hannah and Katie.

"Don't apologize, Tabs," Katie said, striding across to the bench and picking up one of the cellophane packets dotted around the benches. "I think it's lush."

"As I told your dad, there's no danger of your getting lost in the fog in this!" Hannah added.

I was so shocked that they already knew about

this disaster that I found my voice again. "You can't be serious!" I gasped. "You *are* going to make him take them back, aren't you?"

Hannah looked at me as if I'd said something outrageous. "Of course we're not asking Mr Shah to take them back. They're just the job. No one else in the league plays in this colour."

"Course they don't! It's football, not sissy cheerleading!"

"Don't be like that, JJ, please," Katie told me.

Like what? Like anyone in their right mind? "Well, I'm not wearing it. I'd rather die first," I said and slumped down in the far corner, waiting for everyone else to arrive.

Like at practice, they all seemed to turn up at once. From my corner, I watched eagerly for reactions, especially Megan's. Megan was the captain. She had clout. She'd put an end to this. First, her jaw dropped, like I knew it would. Then she grabbed Petra's shoulder, as if to stop herself from fainting. Even better. "Pink? Say it ain't so, Tabby, say it ain't so!" she wailed.

Tabinda hastily went through her Gwendoline-Palermo twaddle again. To my amazement Megan let go of Petra, nodded and said calmly, "Oh, OK. Fair enough." Fair enough? FAIR ENOUGH? She couldn't be serious! Not Megan – she hated girly stuff as much as I did.

Lucy, Eve and Gemma weren't so impressed either, judging from their expressions, but they did the same as Megan; just shrugged and got changed. Course Minter nearly wet herself with joy.

"It's soooooo dreamy! I adore it!" she squealed.

"Me too," Holly gushed. I was really beginning to worry about her.

"Come on, JJ. Time to get ready," Hannah told me when she noticed I was the only one still in my tracksuit.

"I'm not wearing that. I'll just wear my normal strip," I said as calmly as I could.

Hannah shook her head. "Nope."

"Why not?"

"Because I said so."

I glanced round. Everyone was staring. Waiting. Tabinda had her hands over her face as if she couldn't bear it.

"Come on, JJ. It's not the colour that counts – it's what it stands for, right? Us. The Parrs. It's no big deal," Megan said.

"Says who?" I asked, still miffed at how she'd given in so easily. Then I saw why. It was all right for her. She was the goalie. She got to wear yellow. How appropriate.

There was a silence in the changing room; it had built and built without me realizing. You could have heard a pin drop, but I didn't care. I would *not* play in pink. Like I said, I'd rather die first.

Hannah began ushering everybody towards the door, glancing briefly at me over her shoulder. "JJ, if you don't get changed you're on the bench – either that one you've glued yourself to, or the one outside. Up to you."

I didn't move a muscle.

"Oh, here we go again," I overheard Eve say to Gemma as she lined up.

I ignored her and focused on Hannah, hoping she'd smile and say, "Oh, come on, then, I'll let you off this time," but she didn't say anything else, just turned and nodded to Daisy, who was nearest the door. "Let's have you all out on the field now, girls," she said.

And they all trooped out, leaving me to it.

We won four–one. Apparently. I don't know who scored. It's hard to see play when you're three hundred metres away and there's a brick wall with a muddy window in front of you. I didn't feel like joining in the conversation on the journey back, either. There was what you might call a bit of an atmosphere. Hannah tried at first. Asked me if I'd "come round yet" like I'd been in a coma or something.

Katie was a bit more understanding, saying she

knew how I felt. "I've never been a girly-girl, either, but at the end of the day it *is* just a colour..."

That was where she was wrong. Pink wasn't *just* a colour. Not to me, at any rate. It was much more than that. The trouble was I didn't know why it was much more than that. So I just sat there, confused and fuming at the same time.

When they dropped me back at the house, I said thank you very much for the lift and got out of the car, without waving or standing there for ages wishing I could live with one or other of them like I usually did.

I couldn't even make myself look out of my bedroom window when I got in. I kept the curtains shut and sulked right through to Monday.

6

Monday was never going to turn out well, so when Mrs Law dumped a box full of beige-coloured solid shapes on my table and Ronnie the scab-picker with it, I knew it would end in trouble.

"What I'd like you two to do is to identify as many of these shapes as possible. If you get more than six, you'll win an award," Mrs Law trilled.

"What award?" Ronnie asked instantly.

"Ooh. Let's see. How about five points towards a McDonald's voucher each?"

Big wow, I thought, but Ronnie wriggled in his seat. I got the impression he was up for it. Let's face it, a Big Mac had to be better than what he'd been snacking on so far.

He glanced sideways at me. "You going to write 'em down, then?" he asked bluntly.

"Nope," I said. I wasn't in a writing mood. I was in a foot-tapping mood. I do that when I'm unsettled. Tap my feet. Shuffle round. Get agitated. I ignored Ronnie and the box of shapes and thought back to what had happened on Saturday instead. Pink. Of all the colours...

"Stop it," Ronnie grumbled, picking up a cuboid, staring at it blankly for a second, then putting it back down again.

"Stop what?"

"With yer feet. 'S annoying."

I kept tapping. Four–one. Four–one. So Megan hadn't kept a clean sheet, then. I bet that number 21 scored for Hixton. Bet you anything. She wouldn't have scored if I'd been playing. No chance. I'd have marked her closer than Blu-Tack on a poster, I would. My feet tapped harder and harder as I became more and more frustrated. Why did Gwendoline have to be your favourite sweet pea, Mr Shah? I'd checked them out on my computer and there were loads of other varieties he could have gone for that weren't pink. Windsor, for instance. Windsor was a decent claret colour, like Burnley played in, or West Ham.

It was ages before I became aware of a sort of "grrr"ing near me, like the sound a dog makes when it sees the postie coming down the path. The "grrr"ing was coming from Ronnie. "Pack it in, ugly. Or else," he said through clenched teeth when I scowled at him.

It wasn't the "ugly" that got me. I am ugly. So what? It was the "or else". Our Billy says "or else", and it's like being told you're going to get a smack but not knowing when. I hate that. I'd rather have the smack right then and get it over with.

But Ronnie wasn't our Billy. He was just a ten-year-old kid in a mucky Arsenal shirt and I couldn't give a crusty kebab about *his* "or else". I glared at him and as I glared, the mucky red of his shirt turned to a vivid, garish pink. Anger darted through me, fast, furious, and catching me out with its intensity like it always does, so that I had to concentrate on the emblem to stop myself from shaking. "What you wearing that shirt for?" I hissed at him, my fists clenched. "I bet you don't even know who they are."

He began frantically picking at a fresh scab with his blackened fingernails. "Course I do," he snivelled.

"Can you name the manager?"

"Could if I wanted."

"Go on, then."

"Don't want to, do I?"

"That means no. Can you name your top goal-scorer?" I challenged.

I knew I was being nasty, but I couldn't stop myself. I was like a car on the edge of a cliff with the handbrake off.

So was Ronnie. A flash of his hands and the box of shapes was sent crashing onto the carpet. The pieces scattered everywhere. "Parky's off on one!"

someone shouted just as Ronnie lunged at me, his face radish red, his arms outstretched like a zombie's.

I was too quick for him, though, and dodged out of the way easy. "Glory supporter!" I yelled, ducking round the other side of the table and tipping it up on its side like a shield. "Come on, then! Come and get me if you dare!" My breathing was short and hollow in my chest, my stomach was somersaulting, and all I could see in front of me was thick, pink fog.

Before Ronnie could take up my dare, Mr Upton somehow managed to pin his arms to his sides and march him into the corridor while Ronnie screamed words to make your hair curl.

Mrs Law was left to sort the rest of us. "All right, folks, show's over," she said, her eyes flicking from me to the four others in turn, like a lion-tamer not sure which lion's going to leap next. It wouldn't be me. I'd had my blow-out and all I wanted to do was creep into a corner and sleep.

"Good scrap," Clayton White complimented me as I righted my table.

Not long after, Mrs Kelly stuck her head round the door and crooked her finger in my direction. "May I see you in my office, please, Jenny-Jane?" she said ever-so-politely.

When we got there, I told her word for word what had happened.

"Well, thank you for your honesty," she acknowledged, looking up from the notes she'd been making.

"Why, what did glory boy say?" I asked out of curiosity.

"Ronnie? I'm afraid I won't get much out of Ronnie for a while. Mr Upton's still trying to calm him down."

"Oh," I said.

Mrs Kelly tapped her pen on her desk. "Did anything happen before the incident, Jenny-Jane?"

"How do you mean, Miss?"

"What happened to make you so annoyed with Ronnie? To wind him up like that?"

"Nothing."

"Had you had an argument at home, perhaps?"

Like I'd tell her if I had. "No."

"I'm not being nosy, Jenny-Jane, it's just that when people lose their temper at one thing it's often because of something entirely different."

"Nope. Nothing happened earlier."

Mrs Kelly shook her head. "So all this was about a football shirt?"

"Yes," I said truthfully. "It was."

Ronnie didn't come back to class for the rest of the day. Turns out when he loses it, he loses it. "You won't see him for months," Clayton told me at lunch. Suits me, I thought.

7

To make my day even more perfect, only Billy and Brendan were there to greet me when I got home. Apparently Dad had taken Mam to the supermarket as a special treat. "The lazy mare didn't even leave us any sarnies," Brendan complained.

"That's all right. We've got our little sis home now," Billy said. "I'll have ham and pickle, sweetheart."

"Same here," Brendan added. "Two rounds."

"Get lost," I said. I didn't care if I got a clip round the ear for being cheeky. I was that cheesed off I probably wouldn't even feel it.

To my surprise, they both just threw back their heads and started laughing so much I thought their Adam's apples would seize up. After about five minutes, Brendan slid a pound coin over to Billy. "You win," he said.

"Course I do," Billy replied, flicking the coin in the air before pocketing it.

"You had a bet on whether I'd make you a sandwich?" I asked.

"We did."

"You're weird."

Another surprise: he agreed. "That's us. The weird and wacky Bayliss brothers."

"Tell us about your day, JJ," Brendan chipped in cheerfully. "We've had a good one. First we signed on..."

"Which is always a riot," Billy sniffled.

"Then we bumped into some old pals of ours, who asked us to store a few items for them for a little while..."

"In exchange for a few quid, of course," Billy added, sounding more upbeat than he had in months.

"Cool," I said, knowing that meant there'd be

money coming into the house. "What items?"

Brendan wordlessly slid a silver iPhone out from behind the biscuit barrel.

I whistled, knowing it was top range. "Quality," I told him, sliding it back.

"Have it. We've both got one."

"Thanks," I said, and hid it away in my bag.

"Don't flash it about just yet, mind."

"I won't."

"Best make yourself scarce tomorrow tea-time, too. They're dropping the stuff off then and don't want an audience."

"Don't worry, I've got footy practice," I reassured him.

I waited for our Billy to make some sarky comment, but he didn't. What he did was pull out the chair next to him and pat it. "Come on, Jenno. Sit. Take a load off. Tell us about the unit."

"Why?" I asked suspiciously, remaining where I was.

"We're interested."

"Yeah. We're interested. Even *we* never ended up in a unit." Brendan laughed.

I shrugged. "It's the same as everywhere else," I said. "Full of people bossing you about and telling you to do things you don't want to do."

"Ha! Sounds like the dole office!" Billy replied good-humouredly. He took a drag of his cigarette and blew smoke high up to the ceiling. "'Mr Bayliss, we need to see some evidence that you are actively seeking employment,'" he quoted in a high, silly voice. "'Have you thought about warehouse work? There are temporary jobs going.'"

"And what was it you said to her?" Brendan asked.

"I said, 'I've thought about it, duck, but last time I did a warehouse job I ended up in the nick.'"

Billy and Brendan both thought that was hilarious and began hooting and slapping the edge of the table.

"Classic! Classic!" Brendan cried, flinging his

mug in the air and sending frothy amber liquid cascading down the sides.

I rolled my eyes then. It wasn't tea they were drinking, but beer. So that was why he and Billy were being so friendly. They were sloshed. I might have guessed.

"See you later," I said, and left them to it.

8

I didn't sleep much that night, and it wasn't just because of the racket my boozing brothers were making. Every time I dozed off I saw these beige cuboids flying around everywhere, or else I got these stomach cramps that made me curl up in a tight ball.

Next morning the cuboids had gone, but the cramps hadn't. I thought about asking Mam if I could stay home, but I knew Billy and Brendan would have hangovers and I'd rather face twenty zombie Ronnies than the pair of them with splitting headaches.

Luckily, Mrs Law didn't attempt to make me "mix" and Ronnie didn't show, which meant I was left in peace. In fact, I had a half-decent day in the end, so I wondered why I still had stomach cramps when I got home.

It wasn't until I tramped upstairs and drew back the bedroom curtains I'd kept shut since Saturday that it dawned on me. I had cramps because I was worried about going to training.

I gazed out over the main pitch, dappled in late-afternoon sun. It looked like it always did, welcoming and inviting. I held my head up and stuck my chin out. I wasn't going to miss training just because I'd been the only one with the guts to say something about the away kit. Why should I?

So I set off even earlier than normal. I almost wore the yellow nap off my tennis ball, I worked it so hard. When I heard Hannah's car, I stopped and strolled casually across the field, whistling softly like I didn't have a care in the world, though the cramps were snatching at my belly like nobody's business.

Hannah and Katie were about to unlock the

equipment shed. "Here she is, the early girly." Katie smiled as usual.

"Miss Keen," Hannah said, pulling back the door and disappearing inside, only to emerge a second later with a set of slalom poles, which she handed to Katie. "For the first drill," she told her. "About two metres apart to start with."

"Got you." Katie nodded and strode away towards the training pitch.

"JJ, you grab some of these cones," Hannah said to me.

"OK, boss."

As she slid them over to me with her foot, Hannah cleared her throat. "So, calmed down now, have we?" she asked.

"Yep," I replied.

"Sure?"

"Uh-huh."

"Sure you're sure?"

"Uh-huh."

"Good – because you know, JJ, sometimes you

have to decide which battles are worth fighting and which ones aren't, and missing a match because of the colour of your away strip is one that isn't. OK?"

"I guess," I muttered.

"You don't sound convinced."

"But it's pink," I said.

"That's irrelevant, JJ," Hannah replied. "The bottom line is that you put aside your opinions and get on with it for the team's sake. Like Megan did. Yes?"

"Yes," I mumbled.

"Good, because I'd hate to think of you on that bench every week."

"Would you really do that?" I gasped. "You'd drop me?"

She looked at me and nodded. "Yes, I would."

I felt as if I'd been plunged into a fish tank full of electric eels and they were all taking tiny bites out of my skin. "But I'm a good player."

Hannah rapped her knuckles lightly on my forehead. "Hello? Is anyone in there? This season is all about playing as a team, and there's no 'I' in 'team', as the cliché goes."

"I know, but…"

"No, you don't, or we wouldn't be having this conversation. Remember how Petra said we were days of the week?"

"Mmm."

"Well, you were meant to be my Wednesday against Hixton Lees, bang in the middle."

"Oh."

"We needed your fighting spirit, especially in the second half. You were missed."

I stared down at the dusty floor of the shed. I hadn't really thought of it like that. Them missing me. I'm not used to being missed by anyone.

Hannah reached behind my head and lifted the set of hoops off their hook. "So, are you ready to try again?" she asked.

"Yep," I said. "I'm ready."

"Awesome. You can start by putting those cones out!"

As I trundled to the field with the stack of cones, I realized I felt different. The stomach cramps had almost disappeared. Instead I felt all pumped up, because Hannah had made everything better. She'd explained things in a way that made sense, so I could see a reason for them. No lame targets like the ones Mrs Kelly set. No bribing me to do things like Mam does.

When people began to arrive, I wanted to run up to them and say something about Saturday. To tell Tabinda I was sorry for overreacting. To tell Megan I'd been out of order for having a go at her, too. To tell everyone thanks for missing me. But I just couldn't do it. It felt too weird. Instead I worked really, really hard.

If I messed up on the quick-step ladders, I went back and did the exercise again until I got it perfect. If I touched one of the poles during the slalom drill, I went back and repeated the run until I aced it. During the short match at the end, I bet I covered every blade of grass on that playing area, I was so determined to show Hannah how much I cared and how much I wanted to play for the Parrs. I'd be any day of the week she wanted me to be.

In the end, it was one of the best training sessions I'd ever had.

I arrived home feeling all bouncy. "Evenin' all!" I called out, banging the kitchen door and getting a scowl from Mam, who was watching *Holby City*, and a frown from Billy, who wasn't. He was just staring into space, smoking. "Where're Dad and Bren?" I asked.

"Putting something in the shed," Mam said in a hushed voice.

"Oh, yeah! The stuff! That iPhone's ace." I stood on tiptoes and glanced out of the window. Bren was almost collapsing under the weight of boxes in his arms, and a fat bloke with a bald head kept giving him more.

"Don't look!" Mam barked.

"I'm not," I said cheerfully, filling a glass with water from the tap and remembering how smoothly I'd taken the ball round the slalom course during that last drill. I downed the water in one, and was just about to rinse the glass out when I felt a sharp slap on the back of my head. I dropped the glass; it fell with a clatter into the sink. "Ouch! What was that for?" I cried, turning to stare at Billy, already knowing it was him.

"For not listening to what you've been told, laddie-lass. Start flaming listening or else."

"I *was* listening. I was just getting some water," I protested.

He raised his hand again. "Do you want another?"

"Mam!"

"Don't bring me into this," she said, turning the telly up louder.

I glared at Billy before galloping up to my room. One day, I thought, rubbing the back of my head. One day.

9

Ditto what I said last time about the rest of the week. Got up, went to the unit, came home, Billy was Billy, Mam was Mam … blah-blah-blah. Moving on to the good part: Saturday. Parrs v. Cuddlethorpe Tigers. 10.30 kick-off. No tickets required.

The Cuddlethorpe Tigers were nothing special. The only thing that I remembered from last time we'd played them (and beaten them 4–1) was that one of the players was called Serena. I only remembered that because her dad had shouted her name out when she messed up, and the others had gone on about how awful he was – but I'd just thought, why was that awful? At least he cared enough to shout. My dad couldn't even be bothered to get out of bed, let alone turn up to a match.

Anyway, I arrived at the ground well early
– at just gone nine. After I'd jogged round the
field a couple of times and done a few muscle
stretches, I got out my tennis ball and practised
with that.

Eventually I became aware of other people
arriving. In the distance I saw Hannah and Katie
dragging out the goalposts, then Holly and Lucy
and Nika helping to erect them. Every time I looked
across, more people had arrived. When I saw Katie
dump a net full of balls by the touchline, I dashed
across to grab one for myself.

"Morning JJ." She grinned at me.

"OK, boss," I said, then hiked over to a
spot furthest away from everyone. I practised
quick turns and dribbling with both feet along
the byline, until I was called over to join in the
warm-ups.

Before I knew it, we had two minutes to go and
Hannah was gathering us round for the pre-match
chat. Everybody linked arms round shoulders; and

I huddled up with Nika on my left and Eve on my right and listened.

"OK, then, girls. First home match of the season. Are you up for it?" Hannah asked.

"Yesssssssss!" we cheered.

"Conditions are perfect. Sunny but not in-yer-eyes blinding, slight breeze but not gusty enough to affect the ball."

"In other words, we've no excuse for losing!" Eve joked.

"In other words, I want to see you all moving to the ball and I also want to see evidence of what we've talked about – awareness of one another's positions."

"Give us a nice, fluid passing game, as *our* coach is always telling us," Katie added.

Then came the best part – the bit where Hannah told us who was up first. Feeling a bit queasy, I bowed my head as she listed us. Would she give me a go after last week?

"Petra, I'm putting you in the centre…" she began.

"What? You mean I do the toss-up and everything?" Petra asked, a look of panic on her face.

"Uh-huh."

"Choose to kick off if you win it," Megan advised.

"… and, Jenny-Jane, you're midfield on the right," Hannah continued.

I nodded briskly, not wanting to show how elated I was at being one of the first selected. Midfield on the right. That'd do me. I jogged across the pitch, raring to go.

The Cuddlethorpe centre, looking smart in her blue and white striped shirt, stood opposite Petra. "Er … heads," Petra squeaked when the ref tossed the coin.

It was tails. Cuddlethorpe went for the kick-off, and Petra chose the bottle-bank end to defend first.

The second we kicked off I sprang like a greyhound out of its trap. Ten seconds after that, the one and only Serena, who was way too slow to the ball, gifted me possession.

"Wake up, Serena!" I heard her dad call from the touchline.

Stay asleep, Serena! I thought. I put my head down and dribbled, keeping the ball close to my feet as I pounded down the touchline. I loved running along the channels; it's more of a challenge then – preventing the ball from going out of play while trying to keep possession.

From the corner of my eye I saw Dylan waving at me to pass, but she was so easily bundled off the ball and I couldn't risk it. I pushed on, heading straight at a Tigers defender. Swerving easily round her outstretched boot, I reached the edge of the box in no time. Sometimes the seven-a-side pitch is just too small!

A quick glance told me Petra was in a space quite close by, but there was no point passing if she was so nervous; she'd only bodge it. Instead I stopped, steadied the ball, looked for other options and saw none. I was prepared to push close to the corner flag if I had to, so I could try for a tight angled-cross into the penalty area – but that was when two Cuddlethorpe players arrived out of nowhere. I tried to turn, but they were closing me down good and proper... I blasted the ball at their legs, hoping for a rebound, but it bounced into the path of a third Tiger and she hoofed it down the middle.

I galloped after it, feeling on top of the world.

Football, football, football. Love it, love it, love it.

That was pretty much it for the next ten minutes or so – me going deep when needed, and attacking whenever I got the chance. All credit to them, Cuddlethorpe were really giving us a game. Their number 11 was decent (despite having fat knees), but Holly and Lucy were solid at the back and Megan didn't need to make a save all the time I was on.

Midway through the half, Katie swapped me for Gemma and put Nika on for Petra. I didn't mind too much: Gemma is a class player, miles better than me, and I don't mind admitting it. Every time she has the ball you know something good's going to happen.

And this time was no different. Within five minutes she had forced a few good saves out of their keeper, and then Eve put it wide twice – but by half-time it was still nil–nil. The Tigers had had a couple of corners, but they hadn't converted either. All in all, we shaded it for quality, I reckoned. We were bound to score in the second half. Bound to.

Hannah said as much as we gathered round. "Well done, girls! You're throwing everything at it. Keep doing that and you'll be rewarded for sure. I'm liking what I'm seeing! Super-confident play from you, Petra, and you two, Eve and Tabs. Awesome. Hursty – magic first touch, and, Goose, your header out from that corner saved a dead cert..."

"It did." Megan laughed, hitting Lucy on the back. "I was totally out of position."

"And it was good to see the twins flying down the wings!" Katie beamed at Dylan and Daisy, who giggled into their hands.

"So, all of you, keep doing what you're doing, OK?" Hannah said before turning to me, a huge grin on her face. My heart began racing in expectation. I wondered what she'd say to me! My speed was usually one of the things she pointed out. Or the way I always remembered to fall back into defence once we'd lost the ball. Maybe she'd mention the way I'd used both feet? I was pretty good at that, even if I did say so myself.

But no. That wasn't what she focused on.

"Apart from you, JJ. *Don't* keep doing what you're doing!" That was what she said to me. *Don't keep doing what you're doing.*

She didn't say it in a nasty way. Like I said, there was a smile on her face – but it made a few of the team laugh and that made me prickle. "What do you mean?" I asked grumpily.

She stayed with the easy smile. "JJ, you know what I mean. You didn't pass the ball once in fifteen minutes."

"Course I did," I said.

"No you didn't!" everyone chorused.

"I waited ages and ages," Dylan simpered, "and nothing came."

"Well, I thought I'd passed," I mumbled.

"No you didn't, and you know it," Hannah pursued. "I'm really disappointed in you, JJ. After all we've talked about. You should have grown out of hogging the ball by now."

"But why? What's wrong with being a ball hog?" I asked. I wasn't even trying to be stroppy. I really wanted to know. I'd seen players on telly take the ball from inside their own half, weave round three or four defenders, dummy the goalie and score. They got goal-of-the-month awards for that; *I* got criticized.

"Because simply running at defenders like you do doesn't achieve anything; there's no end product. Good players spend hardly any time on the ball. They pass it as soon as they can, to build up the move, to push the ball forward," Hannah explained.

"Often it comes straight back to them when they do pass," Katie said, as if that was meant to make me feel better.

"But I *like* running with the ball. I like the feeling it gives me... It's..." I stopped. What was it? I wanted to describe it properly. It was important. I didn't want people to keep having a go at me. "I ... I..." I stammered.

One or two of the team became restless as Hannah waited for my answer. Amy stooped to pluck her iPhone out of her kit bag and check her texts. It was the same make as the one Brendan had given me the other day.

"I know!" I said suddenly. "It's the only time I ever have anything that's my own." I paused. That was exactly it! When I had the ball, it was mine. I'd earned it. I deserved it. I hadn't pinched it or been given it on a plate. I had won it fair and square.

I grinned at Hannah, dead chuffed with myself, knowing she'd understand – but Eve interrupted before Hannah could speak. "That's the lamest excuse ever," she said, with this massive over-the-top sigh.

I turned and scowled at her. "You what?"

"You heard. Face it, JJ, you're just greedy. You always are – on and off the pitch."

"What do you mean, 'on and off the pitch'?" I said.

"On the pitch you're greedy for the ball. Off the pitch you're greedy for attention."

"Greedy how?"

She opened her hands wide and turned her head from side to side. "Er … hello? Look around."

I frowned at her. "I'm only trying to explain something. If you give me one minute…"

"Why? Why should I give you one minute?

Why should any of us? We've given you enough minutes! You're such a time-suck, JJ, and it's tedious! But nobody ever says anything. Nooo! Because it's JJ, and she's special somehow, so we all tiptoe round her in case she gets into a strop."

I swallowed hard. She made me sound just like our Billy! "I'm not..." I began – but Eve hadn't finished.

She began reeling off a list of things on her fingers while everyone else watched. "During the tournament you got in a strop because you wanted us to be England and we got Ukraine. Last week it was the pink away strip. Next week it'll be something else. Face it, JJ, you are a born attention-seeker."

"Get lost!" I said, glowering at her. "Attention's the last thing I want. Why do you think I always practise on my own whenever I get the chance? I hate attention."

"Newsflash! When you practise on your own with

your annoying little tennis ball it just makes you stand out more."

"It's not ann—" I began, then stopped. "Does it?" I asked instead.

"Yes!" everyone chorused.

"Course it does," Eve continued, her voice less irritated. "It's like saying, 'Look at me. I'm too good to practise with those inferiors.'"

"What? No..."

But Eve was on a roll and she wasn't going to let me in. "And so does the way you turn up fifty hours before everybody else, and so does your getting a lift with Hannah to away games instead of doubling up with some of us... I mean, if sucking up to the coaches isn't the biggest attention-seeking thing in the world, then what is?"

I couldn't believe my ears. "I don't do that for attention!" I turned to Hannah. "I don't!" I said, my voice high and desperate.

"I know," Hannah said. The whistle blew then,

and she scratched her neck. She looked from me to Eve. "It's time for the second half. We'll discuss this later."

Eve rolled her eyes at Gemma as if to say, "I knew that would happen."

That did my head in! "No! Wait!" I cried as everyone began to trudge back towards the pitch. "You lot want to know why I turn up early, then I'll tell you. I turn up early because I hate being at home, that's why. And I get a lift with Hannah because I didn't think any of you would want me in your car."

"I think we might need a little more time here," Hannah said quietly to Katie, who nodded and ran over to the ref.

"'Scuse me!" Megan said after Katie had gone, reminding me that I'd had lifts with her and her dad in the past.

"You're different," I said to her. "You understand about my family."

"What do you mean?" Holly asked.

Megan began making slashing movements across her throat with her finger, warning me not to say anything – but I didn't care. If Eve and the rest of them wanted reasons, they could have reasons. "Because my family are all burglars," I said, "so I thought you wouldn't want someone like me in your car. I mean, I might pinch your road atlases or something, right?"

Holly's eyes looked as if they were going to shoot out of her head. "Seriously?"

"Seriously. That's what I meant when I said I don't have anything of my own. Most of the stuff I have has been jacked."

"Like Nika's boots?" Amy asked.

"Exactly," I admitted, in a hurry to get back to that light feeling I'd had a few minutes before. "So when I'm on the field and I've got that ball, it feels great. Really great." I breathed out heavily, amazed at myself and turned to Hannah. *I'll start passing,* I was going to say to her. *I'll start as soon as you let me. I don't need to be a ball hog any more, now that I know why I do it.* After that I'd thank Eve, because I hadn't realized about the other stuff, and she was right, dead right, and I'd stop arriving fifty hours early if it annoyed people. I'd even wear the stupid pink girly shirt. I'd...

A smile broke out on my face. I'd mix, Mrs Kelly, I'd mix! I meant it, too.

And if Amy Minter hadn't turned to Nika that second and said those two words, I could have ended my story here and you lot could have gone on to watch *Top Gear* or something.

10

"Told you," Amy said to Nika.

Nika looked at me, then at her boots, then back
at me, confused. "Stolen? But you told me they
had fallen off the back of a lorry!"

"It means the same thing," I explained. "But
don't worry, it was ages ago. Nobody can trace
them…"

"Oh," Nika said, and her expression changed
in the same way the teacher's at King John's had
when she'd come back from lunch and seen me
taking her purse. It was horrible, and my insides
felt as if they were being minced.

I glanced across at Megan, who was shaking
her head from side to side and looking at me
with an *I-did-warn-you* expression in her eyes.
I glanced at Petra next to her – and saw pity in

hers. As for the others, they weren't looking at me at all. They were looking at the grass, at their socks – at anything but me.

I had the weirdest sensation then: of icy water slowly trickling down my back. What had I been thinking, opening my mouth in front of this lot? I mean, if even Nika, whose family were as poor as mine, didn't understand, I had no chance with the rest of them – these nice girls from cosy homes, with parents who kissed them every time they went anywhere and read them bedtime stories and took them shopping for fun... No chance.

I watched hopelessly as Nika collapsed on the grass and began to shake the boots off, her hands fumbling as she tried to undo the laces too quickly.

"Don't," I said, crouching down opposite her. "I want you to keep them... I just wanted to try and explain why I hogged the ball, but I'm not going to hog it any more. I promise I'm not... I'll—"

"No," Nika said, tears splashing down on the grass. "I cannot keep them..."

"But you need them…"

Her eyes flashed angrily at me. "I don't need stolen things. I'd be ashamed to wear them."

The icy cold down my back turned into a burn. "Yeah, you're right," I said, straightening up. "Only scum like me would wear stolen boots. Here, have your rubbish ones back," I spat, levering her comfy old boots off. "And the rest of you snobs can get stuffed too!" I called out for good measure, before turning and belting home where I belonged.

11

Mam was mopping the floor when I stormed in. "Oh, Jenny-Jane, be careful! I've just washed that bit!" she grumbled.

"So what?" I told her and plodded right through. "You can always wash it again. You know how you love washing things!" I slammed the kitchen door behind me.

Upstairs, I turned my TV on. It was some feeble cookery programme. A long-haired bloke was whisking eggs in a bowl. "Make sure you mix them well before folding them into the flour..." he said.

Mix them well. MIX. I couldn't stand that word. So short. So loaded. MIX! Everybody tells you to do it, but nobody tells you how, do they? And when you try, it all goes belly-up. "I'll mix *you* well," I told Hairy Bloke and yanked the plug out from the wall. Then I reached up and flung the left panel of the window as fully open as it would go before returning to the telly and heaving it, bit by bit, off the console beneath and up onto the windowsill. Yes! Let's hear it for the new lightweight plasma screens. Off you go, buddy – and I pushed the TV through the window.

Down, down it fell, straight onto the patio. I leaned out, disappointed to see it had not smashed to smithereens, just landed face down, intact. Amazing. Maybe the PlayStation would smash better. Like when the box of 3D shapes had flown everywhere. That's what I wanted – flying bits! Out the PlayStation went, quickly followed by the Xbox and the DVD player. But none of them smashed to pieces and flew like I wanted them to. One or two bits broke off, but that was all. Disappointing or what?

What next? Oh yeah. The new state-of-the-art just-like-Hannah-Montana-wannabe Amy Minter's iPhone. What did I need that for? It was useless, just like those boots had been. Expensive, flashy, but useless.

I didn't drop the iPhone. I flung it as far as I could, and watched it land with a clunk against the laundry pole and ping off again. Yo! This was the most fun I'd had in ages.

Mam's upturned face suddenly appeared in the garden below me. "Jenny-Jane? What are you doing?"

"I'm doing what you do, Mam! I'm tidying up!" I shouted and chucked the computer screen down at her.

She darted sideways with a yelp. "You just wait, you little madam!" she said angrily, then disappeared inside. Ha! What was she going to do? Get the hoover out?

I looked round my bedroom. What other things had fallen off the back of a lorry so that they could now fall off the back of our house?

Before I could decide, my bedroom door clattered open – and Dad, Billy and Brendan were standing there, looking idiotic in their pyjamas with their sticky-up hair. Typical. Half the day gone and they'd only just got out of bed.

"What's going on here?" Billy demanded, a deep frown on his face as he looked round at the mess.

"Don't come near me. Don't you dare come near me!" I growled.

"Come near you? You'd better pray we don't!" Dad said, his frown matching Billy's.

"You should see the stuff outside!" I heard Mam say from somewhere behind them.

They all glowered at me, waiting for an explanation. I knew I was in for it. Without thinking I edged backwards and clambered up onto the windowsill. There I sat, with my backside sticking into the fresh air, my hands clasped on the metal frame. I leaned right back and put my head fully out of the window, gazing up at the guttering for a second before feeling dizzy and ducking back inside.

"Get down from there, you stupid brat," Billy ordered.

I ignored him and stayed exactly where I was. Who cared what he – or any of them – did or said to me now? I'd walked out on the Parrs. Nothing could hurt more than that. "Or else?" I said, and laughed. I saw from his blank expression he hadn't a clue why *that* was funny. I hitched myself further out of the window. The cool breeze travelled up the back of my football shirt, and the sharp edge of the frame bit into my bare legs. I shivered and almost lost my grip. Mam, standing on tiptoes so she could see above Brendan's head, looked alarmed. "Oh my God! Jenny-Jane…"

"Go away, Mam," I told her. "Go and wash some pots."

"Oi! Show your mother some respect," Billy told me.

Respect – I hated that word. What did it even mean? Nothing, coming from him. "What? Like you do? You treat her like a slave. All of you do. 'Fetch me this.' 'Make me that...'" I stopped, as I realized something massive and momentous for the second time that day. "That's why I hate pink!" I cried.

They all looked blankly at each other.

"I hate pink because pink means being a girl," I explained. "And who wants to be a girl in this family when you grow up to be a slave like Mam?"

"Who says *you're* going to grow up at all?" Billy sneered.

"Suits me!" I sneered right back and squeezed my eyes shut until Billy was just a tiny speck. "I can't stand you!" I told him. "You don't have a job. You don't have any friends. You don't have a life – so you take it out on us, you big bully! The only time you're nice is when you're drunk!"

"Oh, you are just asking for it!" Billy yelled and sprang towards me – but Brendan grabbed him.

"No!" he shouted.

"Gerroff," Billy replied, trying to shrug him off.

You're not going to believe what happened then. Brendan – our skinny little Brendan – only got Billy in an arm-lock! A tight one as well, from the look on Billy's face. "Move and I'll break it," he hissed in Billy's ear.

"As if," Billy retorted.

"I mean it, mate. Look at her! Nine years old and about to top herself…"

I frowned then. Top myself? Brendan, you thicko, I thought, I'm not going to top myself.

His face was pale and drained as he continued talking. "We're meant to watch out for her, aren't we? She's our little sister. But we don't, do we. All we've done is make her as bad as us." He raised his head and tried to give me a smile. "It's all right, Jen. You can come down. Nobody'll hurt you."

"Yeah, right. I've heard that one before," I told him, nodding at Billy. I still couldn't quite believe what I was seeing.

"Mam," Brendan hissed, "*do* something."

Mam looked panicked. Her hand was snatching at her hair as if she were plucking a chicken. "Me?

I don't know what to do. I've never known how to handle her."

I turned to her. "Why not? I'm not *that* bad."

Her shoulders sagged. "I suppose I'm just better with boys."

"Well, you did have three of 'em," Billy muttered.

"What's that supposed to mean? That I'm a boy too? If that's your way of having another go at me for playing footy I've got some bad news for you, bro," I told him, jumping down from the windowsill. "I've jacked it in, so you're going to have to find something else to wind me up about." I plonked myself on my bed and began peeling off my socks.

"Eh? But you love football!" Brendan said, releasing Billy.

I began to pick bits of grass and grit from my socks. "I did love it, but it was never going to last, was it. I'm a Bayliss, aren't I? And everyone knows that in the end being a Bayliss is the kiss of death to anything decent, isn't it."

"What do you mean?" Dad asked.

"Nothing," I said.

"No," Dad said, puffing out his chest. "I want to know what you mean about being a Bayliss, because let me tell you there is nothing wrong with being a Bayliss. We go back hundreds of years, we do – unlike half the riff-raff in this country nowadays."

I stared at my socks in silence.

"Jenny-Jane," Dad said sharply, "explain yourself! What do you mean?"

Annoying tears pricked my eyes. "I mean they've found out the truth, haven't they? They know what a nasty piece of work I am and don't want anything to do with me."

"Who told you that?" Billy demanded. "Who said you were a nasty piece of work? I'll do them! Nobody says stuff like that about my sister!"

"Eh?" I looked at him in astonishment.

"Too right," Brendan said. The two of them stood side by side like a pair of scruffy commandos.

That's what's mad about having brothers like mine. They're clipping you round the head one minute and ready to kill for you the next. No wonder I get confused. I rolled my socks into a neat ball. "Thanks," I said, my voice too wobbly to talk for much longer, "but you're all right. I'll cope. I always do, don't I?"

12

After they'd gone, I glanced round at one of the few things I hadn't chucked out of my bedroom window – my alarm clock.

It was bang on twelve. The match would be over. Everyone would have got into their cars, ready for the next part of their Saturday. Holly would be on her way to the Leicester City match with her dad, Lucy would be going into town with her dad and Nika would be off home to her family, to tell them what a horrible person I was…

A lump the size of a tennis ball came to my throat. I hated the thought of Nika doing that. Quickly pulling on my jeans and England shirt, I put my Parrs kit in a Tesco carrier bag and trundled downstairs. I felt a bit jittery, but I knew what the next part of *my* Saturday had to be.

☆ ☆ ☆

The walk to the clubhouse had never seemed so long. My legs felt as if they were treading in treacle. Luckily Mandy was outside the main door, just opening up for lunchtime.

"Hello, sunshine," she said when she saw me.

I wasn't really ready for a chat, even with Mandy, so I thrust the carrier bag at her. "Will you give this to Hannah, please? It isn't washed – but I only wore it for half an hour, so it's not that mucky either."

"Why don't you give it to her yourself? She's still in the changing rooms."

"Oh," I said, taken aback. I hadn't reckoned on any face-to-face stuff.

I headed for the changing rooms. I'd just dump the kit and go. No long speeches to Hannah or any of that malarkey. It'd be too embarrassing. What Eve had said about me sucking up to her and Katie was still making me squirm.

I marched fast, wanting to get the return of the

kit over and done with, but I pulled to a halt as I reached the open door. Hannah wasn't alone. There were loads of voices, all talking over one another. The whole team was in there, from the sound of it. I hesitated outside, not wanting to interrupt the post-match conference. My eyes really stung then, as I realized I didn't even know what the score had been.

I was about to chuck the kit by the door and walk off when I caught the end of something Amy was saying, and froze. "... and she wasn't even ashamed of it. That's the worst part. My mum's shop has been broken into three times this month..."

So this wasn't a post-match conference; it was a post-JJ conference with Minter as chief spokeswoman. This should be good. I edged as close to the doorway as I could without being seen.

"Three times! Do you know how much her insurance premiums have gone up?" Minter continued.

"Enough about your mum's shop!" Eve told her. "We're trying to work out what to do about JJ!"

I nearly burst in and told her not to bother because the attention-seeker had left the building – but I was curious to know what else Hannah Montana had to say before I thumped her.

"I know! That's why I'm mentioning the shop!" Amy ranted on. "JJ giving Nika stolen property makes Nika an accomplice in the eyes of the law. You can ask my mum if you don't believe me. So all I'm saying is I don't think it's right to have someone like that on the team."

"Cobblers! Nika can't get into trouble for not knowing the boots were nicked," Megan told her.

"It was still wrong of JJ to give them to her," Holly said.

"True," Megan said. "But I reckon she was just trying to be kind."

I couldn't believe that Megan was sticking up for me even though I'd been so nasty to her about the away strip. I should have known, though. Megan had always been there for me.

Then Nika began speaking. "I think she was being kind too," she said, her voice still trembling. "And I don't want JJ to leave the team because of this."

I don't know how I kept still behind that door. Now *she* was sticking up for me as well! I was desperate to tell Nika I was sorry about the boots. It had never crossed my mind she could get into trouble.

"But what if she steals something from *us*?" Amy asked now.

"She won't," Megan said firmly.

"How do you know?"

"Simple! She'd have done it by now!"

I couldn't help smiling then. Megan knew me well. I owed her – big time.

"Could I say something?" Lucy asked.

I craned my neck, curious to hear what Lucy would add. She was one of the "always play by

the rules" brigade. I supposed she'd be backing
Amy up.

"Course you can, Goose. That's what we're here
for," Hannah told her.

"Well, this isn't about JJ, exactly – it's about
Lily Parr."

"Lily who?" Amy asked.

"Lily Parr. The woman the team was named
after."

"Oh. Right." You could tell Minter didn't have
a clue.

"Well, my dad bought me a book about her and
the team she played for, the Dick, Kerr's Ladies…"

"And?" Eve asked.

"And Lily Parr pinched things."

"Did she?" Hannah sounded surprised.

"Yes. She had a reputation for it. She nicked stuff
from the landlady in the digs they stayed in. She
pinched the match ball several times by sticking it
up her jumper…"

"No!" Amy squealed.

"It's true. And she smoked and swore and spat a lot, and when she was a kid everyone called her a tomboy because she hated anything girly..."

"Who does that remind you of?" Eve laughed.

"So what are you trying to say, Lucy?" Hannah asked.

"That I agree with Megan. We can't let JJ leave the team because she thinks we look down on her and her family; that'd be awful."

"It would make us snobs, like she said we were," Gemma added.

"Hang on, though. This meeting's not just about the boots, is it – it's about what Eve said to her at half-time, too," Holly pointed out.

"Yeah, but I didn't mean to cause all this..." Eve said.

"Don't back down. You only said what everyone thinks," Holly said.

"Exactly!" Amy agreed.

That started everybody talking over each other again, until Hannah called for hush. "All right, all right!" she said, loud and clear. "We'll be here all day at this rate. Let's leave it until training on Tuesday. If JJ comes to that…"

"She won't," Megan said, her voice flat and defeated.

"Especially as we're away next week," Petra said. "She definitely won't come if she has to wear the pink shirt…"

"Oh, please don't mention the pink shirt!" Tabinda groaned. "Every time I close my eyes I see that look of disgust on JJ's face."

My head dropped. What had I done? I seemed to have upset nearly every member of the team one way or another. I'd messed up, just like I'd messed up at King John's and messed up at the unit. And this time I couldn't blame our Billy or Mam or being a Bayliss. I'd messed up all on my own, by – as Hannah had said the other day – choosing the wrong battles to fight. Well, I didn't want to fight any more. Not against these guys, who stood up for me when they shouldn't, and liked me when there was nothing much to like, and still wanted me in their team after all the mistakes I'd made. If they could do all that for me then it was time I did something for them. Time to become a non-attention-seeking ball-passing pink-wearing ready-to-mix full-on Parr, because otherwise…

I grimaced. I didn't want to think about otherwise.

Realizing they'd probably be spilling out any second, I knew I had to act straight away. I pulled my shoulders back, stuck my chin out and stepped through the door.

Everybody turned. My heart was hammering faster than a fox's trying to cross a motorway, but I knew I mustn't bottle it. Not this time. "Wotcha," I said, planting a grin on my face. "I suppose you got thrashed without me?"

Final Whistle

I'm not going to tell you everything
that happened next. Let's just say
that when I finally arrived back
at the house I had two kits in my
carrier bag — home and away — plus
Nika's old boots, which she insisted
I take back with me. I might also
have had wet eyes and a bit of a
sniffly nose, but that wasn't from
crying because I was so happy that
everything had got sorted. No way!
I just had a bit of a cold coming
on after sitting on that draughty
windowsill, that was all.

   The following Saturday we played
the Furnston Diamonds. Now that
was the tester — because I knew it
wouldn't be my feet that Tabinda and
co. were looking at when I got out

of Megan's car, but my top. Would
I be wearing the pink shirt? Does
Alex Ferguson chew gum? Is Lily Parr
a legend? Yes. Yes. Yes.

And yes, I warmed up with everybody
else, and yes, I passed the ball,
and yes, I got a buzz out of it when
Hannah told everyone at the end of
the match how delighted she was that
we were playing as a team. I was
less chuffed when everyone started
patting my shoulders and ruffling my
hair. Just because I've got my act
together doesn't mean I've turned
soft.

I'm not going to tell you about
the unit, either. Let's just say
my days there are numbered. By the
time you've finished reading this,

I'll have started my placement at
a new primary school. Granted,
it's only two days a week to start
with, and Mr Upton has to accompany
me like some sort of giant hairy
babysitter — but, you know, whatever
it takes to escape from the nutters.

In the end, escaping was easy.
I didn't even know I was doing it.
On the Monday after the Cuddlethorpe
match (3-0 to us, BTW), I stuck
a Toblerone under Ronnie's nose.
"It's a triangular prism," I told
him after he'd stared at it for
about a year. "And this," I said on
the Tuesday, producing a roll of
fruit pastilles, "is a cylinder."
Wednesday was a packet of Smints
(cuboid), and Thursday a Walnut Whip

(almost a pyramid). By Friday I'd
run out of ideas and dosh, but Mrs
Law was chucking points at me left,
right and centre, Ronnie was my new
maths partner — and Mrs Kelly had
called me into her office.

She went, "Well done on meeting
your target, Jenny-Jane."

And I went, "What do you mean?
I only gave Ronnie a few sweets."

And she went, with a smile on
her face the size of Switzerland,
"Exactly."

Strange, but true.

I'm not going to tell you about
home, either. Seriously, I'm not.
There's really no point. Mam's still
Mam. Dad's still Dad. Billy's still
Billy, and Brendan's still Brendan.

They haven't changed. I have,
though. And that's all that counts,
isn't it?

It's Tabinda's turn to tell you
what happened next, so I'll pass you
on to her. PASS. Gerrit?

See ya,
JJ